A HOLLYWOOD KIND OF MURDER

A Walter Anchor Ghost Detective Story, Case #5

ROBERT J. MCCARTER

Little Hummingbird Publishing

A Hollywood Kind of Murder

A Walter Anchor Ghost Detective Story

Copyright © 2020 by Robert J. McCarter

Cover images ©DepositPhoto.com, Buurserstraat38

Version 1.0, July 2020

ISBN: 978-1-941153-42-0

Visit Robert's website at: www.RobertJMcCarter.com

Published by:

Little Hummingbird Publishing

P.O. Box 23518

Flagstaff, AZ 86002

❀ Created with Vellum

- **Case 1: Detecting Haley** (also part of *Life After: Stories of Life, Death, and the Places in Between*)
- **Case 2: The Ghost Bride's Gift**
- **Case 3: A Long Hard Fall**
- **Case 4: Death of a Dentist**
- **Case 5: A Hollywood Kind of a Murder**
- **Case 6: The Red Arrow Murders** (coming September, 2020)
- **Unfinished Business: The Cases of Walter Anchor Ghost Detective** (coming October, 2020)

Chapter One

EMILY TOOK MY HAND AND DRAGGED ME AWAY FROM THE gathering ghosts. Her green eyes in her young face were sparkling and I knew it could mean only one thing. Murder.

A smile played on her lips and her head slowly nodded, her tight blond curls bouncing around her round face. She guided me quickly around the granite gravestones and the ghosts, the noonday sun hanging in the sky above us. A breeze was rattling the leaves of the tall trees that watched over the graveyard and the murmur of ghostly conversation was a pleasant white noise.

Every night at midnight in our Tucson, Arizona, graveyard we ghosts gather and tell stories or put on plays. It is at midnight that the dead feel most alive. We gather to hold our loneliness at bay and to affirm our shared humanity despite our lack of biology.

But lately, we have started to gather at noon, when we feel the weakest and just assemble into groups and talk. It's not a formal gathering like the Midnight Circle, but a natural confluence of need.

The world is starting to believe in us ghosts and that has caused a spectrum of reactions from joy to revulsion, and there have been mumblings among some ghosts that maybe all of this communication with the other side, as ghosts like me write their stories, is not a good thing. That the living should not be concerning themselves with the dead. That we should remain silent and invisible and focus on what we are here to do, namely taking care of our unfinished business.

We are the earth-bound spirits. We all have unfinished business. My name is Walter Anchor and I have more than most. Solving my own murder for starters.

I glanced down at Emily, there was a wicked look on her face. She died when she was four years old, and looks it, but that was eighty-one years ago and she often acts like it.

She is this strange dichotomy, this mixture of youthful enthusiasm and world-weary wisdom. She can be like an excited child one moment and like a wicked old lady the next. You never know which Emily you are going to get.

"What's going on, Emily?" I asked.

Her eyebrows shot up and she jerked her finger to her lips like a librarian scolding a restless boy in a library and kept dragging me forth.

And then I noticed she wasn't wearing her usual blue shorts and white T-shirt with a big red lollipop on it. She always wore that outfit, unless it was Christmas when she wore an awful red and white sweater. Emily was wearing a plain black dress that went just past her little knees and had a black ribbon in her hair corralling the blond ringlets.

She was jerking me along, weaving us in and out of the ghosts who were staring at us. I shook my head and focused on keeping up with her, keeping my legs going and not bumping into any other ghosts.

I could have flown, but Emily wouldn't have liked that. It wasn't how we conducted ourselves at the graveyard. We did our best to look and act like we did when we were alive.

Emily had saved my afterlife. She was my best dead friend. And we were ghost detectives, solving murders together, so I felt like I could give her the benefit of the doubt here.

Besides, novelty is always welcome. Since ghosts don't have to spend all that time maintaining their bodies (food, sleep, washing, work, elimination) we have a lot of time on our hands.

"Is it a murder?" I whispered. With Emily it usually is —the girl just loves murder.

Her eyes widened and her lips pursed, so much so that it looked rather comical on her four-year-old face. I chuckled and let her drag me along.

And that chuckle was really needed. I had recently delved deeply into my past and had to confront some uncomfortable realities about how I died. About how fixated I had been on finding my murderer and had blocked out a suspect that might have either done it or been a catalyst. Someone close to me that I didn't want to believe would hurt me.

And I hadn't told Emily because she would want to investigate and I just couldn't face it.

Even though she looked like she was a little girl, Emily was a wise old ghost and she must have known I was holding something back. Things had gotten kind of tense between us. But this was playful and different, so I welcomed it.

"Maybe we should branch out," I said as she dragged me along, getting into the playful spirit of it. "You know, do some spying for the government. 'The case of the missing beryllium' or 'The spatiotemporal anomaly' or some such madness. No. I got it. Let's go to the International Space Station and help with some experiments. They could boost up one of the new smaller SECI chambers and we could chat with them all day."

The SECI chamber is a high-tech typewriter for ghosts that lets me tell you my stories. I know they are working on a version three which won't be a chamber at all, but kind of a really chunky laptop.

Now Emily was just looking mad, her forehead furrowed and her lips forming a pout so I shut up. She wasn't being *that* playful.

But I am a detective now, not an actor or a dentist like I was when I was alive, so I started detecting.

First the unusual clothing. She looked like she could be dressed for a wedding or a funeral or church in the long-sleeved black dress. Her feet were bare, but they were always bare. For a ghost, shoes don't serve a functional purpose, especially if you died at the age of four in 1931.

Next was her being so mysterious. Why drag me through the graveyard when she could have just grabbed my hand and popped me away? "Popping" is what we call it when a ghost instantly goes from one place to another. It's an advanced skill that not all ghosts can do.

Did she want all the other ghosts to see us? Did she want me to wonder? Was this driven by a playful four-year-old or a wily ghost over eighty years dead?

Our last case had resolved nicely, no loose ends, so it couldn't be that.

When we were well away from the other ghosts but still in the graveyard, she stopped and let go of my hand and looked me up and down. I was a dentist when I died, and having spent most of the last ten years of my life in scrubs, that's what my ghostly form looked like. After we solved our first case, the murder of Haley, a dental assistant that had worked at my practice, Emily had talked me into changing my ghostly appearance into something more appropriate to our chosen line of work in the afterlife.

So she was looking at my trench coat and fedora, which looked just like Humphrey Bogart's in *Casablanca*. It worked for Emily because of her age and this is how she thought a detective should look. It worked for me because I had tried to make a go of it as an actor and loved those old movies. Besides, this outfit has a definite noir feel to it and that reflects my view of this afterlife.

"Change into something more appropriate," Emily said, pointing at her black dress.

Now this is not an easy thing to do. It took a lot of practicing to go from scrubs to a trench coat and hold it steadily. But I am an actor and I found that I have some affinity for "costume" changes when the need arises. I can't always hold them for very long, but I can do it.

It's been very useful when we have interviewed ghosts for our cases. Being "dressed" in a familiar way is essential if you want to talk to a new ghost. They are easily spooked.

Yeah, I know. That joke was kinda lame, but I gotta try. Can't let all this afterlife stuff get too heavy. Not all the time, at least.

"Why?" I asked, crossing my arms. This was all fun and games, but a costume change was still work and I didn't have a clue what was going on.

"Because," she said with a twist of her mouth, in full-on defiant four-year-old mode. She crossed her arms to match mine and copied my rather stiff posture.

Like I said, things had gotten rather tense between us because of the secret I wasn't sharing and we weren't talking about.

I sighed and nodded my head, letting the fedora

dissolve away revealing my curly black hair. I didn't wear the hat all the time—being up on my head it's hard to know if I have it right. So that was easy.

I looked down at my trench coat and turned it from tan to black. A small change that I could manage easily. "There," I said.

Her arms still crossed, she shook her head. I could do better and she knew it.

This wasn't fun anymore, but I felt guilty about how things were between us, so I kept going. I shortened the trench coat to just below my waist showing black slacks. I pulled in the lapels and made my tie plain and black.

It was a lot to hold, a lot to think about it, but I could maintain it as long as I didn't have to think about much else. Honestly, my little costume trick is linked to me being in a role. If I get into the head of being a butler, I can look like a butler. I had no role here, so it was hard and I was sticking close to my default form.

The trench coat was my default form since I had held it for so long, so if my concentration broke, it would pop back.

The coat wasn't quite right, it was still too baggy, the lapels still too big, but it wasn't half bad. I was rather pleased with the effort.

"I guess that'll do," Emily said, but she looked rather resigned.

I opened my mouth to ask her what was going on, but then closed it. She wasn't in the mood to tell me, but this whole outfit change led me to believe this was something important to her. Something personal. Something she didn't want to involve the rest of the graveyard in. Something sudden and unexpected.

She grabbed my arm and with a "pop" we were gone.

Chapter Two

THE DEAD ARE INTO ALL KINDS OF THINGS THAT HELP them pass the slow progression of time. Some spend their days at funerals, others spend their nights at clubs. Some are obsessed with weddings, others haunt hospitals and wait to greet the newly dead. Some know the TV schedule and which house usually has on the shows they like. Some haunt theatres and put on performances right next to the living and some are in the audience watching. Some travel and see the world.

Many end up haunting the ones they left behind or a place that was important to them and can't leave. I did both before Emily found me. And most of them end up trapped in a place filled with their own regrets we call the bardo. Emily saved me from the bardo.

No body means no job, no eating, no need for shelter, and nothing to buy. And all those things mean you have a lot of time. You have to fill it. The Midnight Circle is one way we ghosts do that. It's our social time where our community gathers.

And Emily, having been dead for over eighty years and

not fallen to the bardo, must have developed some great ways to pass the time. With us, though, it's always been solving murders.

It never occurred to me that Emily had another pastime. I mean, we weren't always together or anything. She was off doing things all the time. But I looked at her as the murder girl. The ghost that found me right before I fell into the bardo, who said she could smell murder even though ghosts have no sense of smell.

And that thought makes me feel guilty. Emily found me, trained me to be a proper ghost, helped me find something worth doing in this afterlife, and I didn't know nearly enough about her. Looking back and writing from where I am now, I feel terrible about this. I had let our relationship be all about me.

Sure, at the time, it felt like Emily was just dragging me from murder to murder because that was her thing, but I know better now. I know she was doing it for me, to keep me busy, to keep me from losing myself in my regrets and falling into the bardo. She was trying to help me do the thing I said I wanted to do the most. Find my own murderer. And here I was holding out on her.

But this is all hindsight. And this kind of rumination can quickly become unhealthy if you don't learn your lessons and move on—whether you are dead or alive.

And I'm here writing about all of this because I want to learn my lessons. I want to be a better ghost and a better friend. I want my afterlife to have purpose and meaning.

That day, though, Emily popped us to a funeral.

It was an open casket affair in a wood-paneled room that looked like it belonged to an upscale mortuary. The coffin was brightly polished wood with ostentatious flower arrangements flanking both sides. Behind it was a strip of stained glass with a prominent cross in the middle, bright light streaming in. The grieving widow was dressed all in black weeping in front of the coffin. She was in her fifties, but with a beautiful face, the crow's feet and laugh lines only serving to make her more appealing. She had blond hair and bright blue eyes.

I couldn't stop looking at her.

"Tony, Tony, Tony," she said, dabbing at her eyes carefully with her handkerchief. She had a thick Boston accent. "Why'd you go and do it? Why'd you take him on? You knew it would end with a bullet in your heart. You knew you'd leave me here alone. What? I wasn't pretty enough or young enough for you anymore?"

Something tickled at my brain about her. She was familiar. There was something about her little speech that was off, but I couldn't look away. In the casket was a handsome man in his sixties with a cleft chin and greying black hair dressed in a very expensive black suit, his skin grey.

The widow's upper lip trembled as she stared at the man, her face going from sad to angry in a heartbeat, her cheeks flushing red. "I knew about the affairs, Tony!" she spat. "Of course, I knew about the affairs. But I—"

"Cut!" another voice shouted and the woman stepped back and looked around, the anger draining from her lovely face. I looked around too.

We weren't in a funeral home, we were on a set, the façade of the funeral home only went back twelve feet. I looked down at Emily and she smiled, a wicked glint in her green eyes.

"Okay, Sheila," the voice said. It belonged to a thin man of about thirty with sandy blond hair and a lean athletic build. He had a beanie containing his hair and one of those annoying ultrashort beards. He looked like he belonged in Hollywood and I instantly disliked him. "That was perfect. We're going to pull the cameras in and do it all over and get some closeups."

Shelia… I did know the woman. She was Shelia Green and had been on a daytime soap for over twenty years. *The Wild and the Willing.*

I had worked with her on a play way back when. She was a diva if ever there was one.

My nonexistent stomach clenched. We were in Hollywood, where I had failed as an actor, where I had found the love of my life, married her, and then lost her before I went running back to Tucson to become a dentist.

I'd only been in Hollywood once since I died. I didn't want to be in Hollywood.

"What the hell are we doing here?" I asked Emily, my voice coming out harsher than I intended.

"Wait for it…" she said, her right eyebrow arched, her nose wiggling like she was sniffing something, completely oblivious to my tone. She was telling me that she "smelled" murder.

"How much longer, Alvin?" Shelia asked the young director, her Boston accent was gone and she looked bored. People swarmed the set and moved around equipment. They were the grips. This was the job I did after acting petered out and while I was working my way through college and dental school. "I've got a Pilates appointment I just can't miss."

"Not long," Alvin said with a smile. "We'll get you out of here on time."

Shelia rolled her eyes as soon as Alvin turned his back and leaned against the coffin. "You can move, you know," she said to the corpse. "Jesus Christ, Eddie, are you sleeping on the job?"

"Wait for it…" Emily whispered again.

The actress sighed and looked around at the organized

chaos. Lights were being moved, perched on tall stands. Cameras and cables and sound gear, too. At a glance it looked like madness, but each person knew what they were doing and moved swiftly and quietly. Time was money and the crew acted like it.

I liked being a grip. I liked still being in the action even if it did make my heart ache to always be on the wrong end of the camera.

Shelia turned back to the casket. "Enough, Eddie. Really!" She poked the man in the casket once and then twice and then she leaned close. "Eddie...?"

I glanced at Emily and she had on a huge thousand-watt smile. I looked back at the casket where Shelia was gently touching the man's face. "Oh... I.... You... your skin is cool." And then her voice rose into a shout. "Eddie! Oh my God, Eddie!"

Shelia Green screamed and all that activity stopped.

"He's dead?" I asked Emily quietly. Being back in Hollywood and popping onto a set that looked like a funeral home but was not with an actor that was really dead, not just faking it, was messing with my mind. I felt like I could barely think.

"He's dead," Emily repeated gleefully. "So dead."

"Murder?" I asked.

"Oh, yeah," she said.

I nodded and flew straight up. I had to get out of there. It was too much. Solving murders in Tucson was one thing, but here in the land of dreams where I had lost everything was... well, it was too much.

Chapter Three

EMILY DID THIS ONCE BEFORE. SHE FOUND A DEAD BRIDE alone in a bridal suite who looked a lot like my ex-wife. She thought I would love it. I lost it.

It's the nature of Emily, sometimes she miscalculates things like this. Badly. She was four when she died. She learned most all of what she knows about the living while dead. She learned by observing the living, not actually living.

And that is not to say that she isn't pretty shrewd about the human experience at times, it's just kind of hit and miss.

And this was a huge miss for me.

I paced the massive curved roof of the soundstage on the Warner Brothers lot. The hum of the Ventura Freeway was to the north of me and the bushy Mount Sinai rose to the east and the Hollywood hills to the south. The sky was clear, a washed-out blue, and the sun hung right above me, not providing me with the warmth or comfort it did when I was alive.

I had been on this lot. I had worked in the soundstage

below me on both sides of the camera. I had lived with my ex-wife Sun a few miles to the west of here.

I was upset, but I didn't fly away. I just paced. And I did it right. One step at a time, with intent. Trying to act as if I was living, like I had a body, trying to calm myself down and keep my ghostly form firm.

The roof was a dirty grey and showing its age. The grunge of it hiding the glossy illusions made right below it. Except the guy in the coffin was really dead. That was no illusion.

This was my old world and my new world colliding. The acting life I had, that I wanted so much, but couldn't keep. And the afterlife I was living with Emily trying to solve murders. Trying to solve my own murder.

It didn't take long, Emily popped in with a sheepish look on her face.

"What are we doing here, Emily?" I asked.

"What we always do, Walter," she said quietly. "Solving a murder."

"He had a heart attack," I snapped. "He died of natural causes." I just blurted it out, but it made sense. And could be right, ghosts are more than a little bit intuitive.

Emily pointed at her nose and shook her head. "No. I mean, he may have had a heart attack, but if so, someone helped him along."

I stopped and crossed my arms. "Why are we here, Emily? Here. Why not New York or Chicago or London. There are murders everywhere. Why are we *here*?"

Emily licked her lips and nodded, sitting down on the flat strip at the crest of the roof. She was back in her blue shorts and lollipop print T-shirt and I realized I was back in my trench coat. I had lost my focus and my form had reverted, but I didn't care.

I paced some more, and she just sat there placidly

looking out over the city. She was waiting for me to calm down, to sit down. I sighed and sat, but I was anything but calm.

"Ever since you wrote about your last day alive—" she began, taking my hand.

"I've been a miserable bastard," I finished.

She nodded.

Here it was, the moment where I should tell about the lead I had and we could pop off and go investigate my murder again, except... It was too much. I was tired of confronting my past and seeing that it wasn't really what I thought it was. It's like the life I thought I had was crumbling, eroding away every time I looked, and soon it would be nothing that I would even want to remember. For me hindsight and all that twenty-twenty business was just a bitch.

"I'm sorry, Emily," I said. "I... It was a lot harder than I thought reliving all of that."

She nodded and squeezed my hand. She did it right so I felt that ghostly, barely-there sense of touch you can experience as a ghost. "I bet. But I know you aren't telling me something."

I opened up my mouth to speak, but she held up her hand.

"And you get to have your secrets," she continued. "I've got secrets, Walter. Things about my past I'll probably never tell anyone. It's okay. But..." She trailed off, staring up at the pale blue sky and then her green eyes found mine and her round face pulled down into a frown.

It was times like this that I wished Emily looked her age, that it was an old woman sitting across from me. As much time as I've spent with her and as well as I know her, when I look at her my mind still tells me she's a kid.

She shook her head as if clearing her thoughts and

changed her tact. "I think you should stay here, Walter. This was your dream. This was what you wanted. You may not be alive anymore, but you can stay here, you can investigate that death." She nodded down to the roof and the set below us. "You can find a way to do something useful here."

I tried to gather my thoughts. Staying here didn't feel right to me. And I was so curious as to what she had been about to tell me with that "but" and how we all have secrets.

"I know you think I goofed in bringing you here," she said, standing up and brushing her shorts off. The gesture was a lot like Emily. It was a normal thing to do, but only if you had a body and sitting on a roof could actually get you dirty. Emily maintained the illusion of being alive because it helps you feel stable as a ghost. But she went the extra mile with it. Maybe that's one of the reasons why she's managed to be dead for so long and has not fallen into the bardo.

"I didn't goof," she said, standing up straight, her head just above mine since I was still sitting. "I didn't. Looking at your past really socked you, but good. Like a hard smack to the kisser. But you were looking at the past you didn't want, the dentist. Maybe you are meant to be here, a ghost among the actors. You could solve murders or... I don't know... start a gossip column telling all the secrets of the stars, or... something."

She leaned down so we were eye to eye, her green eyes intense. "I just want you to be happy, Walter. Maybe you can find a way to be happy here."

She stood, gave me a wistful smile, and with a "pop" was gone.

Chapter Four

THE SET WAS CHAOS, MORE CHAOTIC THAN ITS USUAL norm, and that was saying something.

Shelia Green was crying as she hauntingly told the police about finding the body, her hand shaking as she pointed back to the set and the coffin. She made it sound like this was the worst thing that had ever happened to her, but I wasn't sure I was buying it.

What I was sure of is that there was some acting involved. Her emotional display was being manipulated, but I couldn't tell how. I was a good enough actor, had done it myself enough, that I could tell she was acting. Now, someone like Meryl Streep, forget it, I would never know. But Shelia Green, yeah, I could tell she was faking this to some degree.

Two paramedics had pulled the corpse out of the coffin, but they were moving slow since there wasn't a life to save. Blue uniformed security guards were doing crowd control, shooing away curious cast and crew. And I hovered over it all. Watching. Listening.

Not because I wanted to. Not because I thought there

was an afterlife for me in Hollywood, but because… Well, I don't really know why.

After Emily popped away, I sat on the roof, my mind not in gear. I was half convinced Emily knew exactly what I was keeping from her. I mean, she got that the end of my life in Tucson had been a failure and it had become more of a failure by going back and remembering it all and reliving it all.

Why didn't I want to follow the lead and see if I could find my murderer? Why? I was scared of confronting more of the reality of my life. Terrified, actually, to see it any clearer. What kind of coward was I?

My life was a shambles those years as a dentist. The gambling problem. The propofol problem. The not moving on from my ex-wife problem. But it was the work that got me through my days. I genuinely liked dentistry. I liked working with my staff—even though there were illegal activities and so much other stuff going on right under my nose that I was clueless about.

And that was why I was hovering over the set, watching the humans swirl, listening to the combined cacophony of all the voices as I hovered above them. I enjoyed my work in the afterlife too. Sure, I would be grumpy every time Emily dragged me away and presented me with a new corpse and a new mystery, but I did like solving cases. Just like with dentistry, it felt like I was doing something good, doing something important.

The clue I found reliving my last day and the haunting of my dental practice was a person. Someone close to me. Someone that might have murdered me or been catalytic in my murder. That was the reality that I couldn't face. That someone I cared about could have done it.

And, yes, I've been a detective long enough to know that is how it usually goes. Most murders are done by someone the victim knows. But that is a dry fact. Facing that reality was something I wasn't ready for.

"Oh no. Oh hell no!" a voice close to me said.

I looked around and found another ghost floating near me. It was a plump woman with bright red hair and brighter lipstick. She had glasses hanging from a chain around her neck and wore a blue pants suit.

"Get on out of here," she said, making a shooing motion with her hands. I noticed that the fingernails were also a bright red. "Darla doesn't need any help. This is my crime scene. My case. Get your trench-coated ass outta my soundstage."

She had red high heels on with her business attire which just struck me as funny given we were floating twenty feet above the floor.

"Hi," I said, extending my hand. "My name is Walter Anchor and I died when someone overdosed me with propofol."

It was the ritual, how a ghost greeted another ghost back in Tucson with our name and how we died. I had done it many times, but this time it felt strange. I wasn't in Tucson and this ghost didn't seem to care.

"I know who you are," she said. "Darla was a big reader when she was alive. Darla read through all your cases, you and the little one that looks like Shirley Temple but is a wicked old thing. But you just go now. This here is my case. I don't need no Walter Anchor to help me out. I don't need no schooling from you."

She flapped her hands at me and my jaw just dropped.

She knew who I was. She didn't want me here. And how did she know about the murder? I looked at the scene below, all the emergency personnel, and saw a policeman on his radio. She had probably been somewhere listening to the police band.

She was glaring at me, her sharp blue eyes embedded in her round face. "Cat got your tongue?" she asked. "Big, strong man afraid of Darla? You run out of murders in Arizona?"

I just stared. I mean, the afterlife has all sorts, but I had never met a big, red-headed, high-heeled woman that speaks of herself in the third person and seems to care more about securing her territory than actually investigating the murder.

I nodded slowly and pointed down at the sniffling Shelia Green. "If this was a murder, I would look into her." Darla opened her mouth to speak, but I held up my hand and stopped her just like Emily had just done with me. "I've worked with her, and right now she's acting. Those tears aren't real." I turned and pointed at the corpse. "The paramedics suspect a heart attack, but Emily was sure this was a murder. Maybe he was poisoned so it will look like a heart attack. If you have anyone that helps you, I would have someone stick with the body so you can get those details."

I smiled at her, as genuinely as my acting skill would allow, and floated up towards the roof. "Nice meeting you, Darla," I called back. "Good luck solving the murder."

Chapter Five

THE TRUTH IS, I WAS FINE WITH SOMEONE ELSE
investigating the murder, if that's what it was. It seemed all
too Hollywood to me. An actor found dead in a coffin
while filming a funeral scene. People could say, "Well, at
least he died with his boots on, doing what he loved."

But I didn't fly east back to Tucson when I got outside.
I looked over the rows of huge soundstages with their
humped roofs and over to Stars Hollow, the bucolic town
square just to the east, and New York Street not far from it,
and the iconic Warner Brothers water tower.

This was where the living made illusions seem real.
This was where I had hoped to spend my life working. And
then it hit me, this combination of excitement and fear
right in the gut. My ex-wife Sun might be here. Right now.
Today. Her police procedural drama was set in LA, and
they sometimes shot on this set.

Sun and I had reconciled, as much as the living and the
dead can, after the case with the ghost bride. I had written
her a few times via the SECI chamber, but I hadn't seen
her again.

There was a lot about the Hollywood life out here that I hated. The constant competition and backstabbing, the vast gulf between the haves and the have-nots, the homeless people and the drug use, the constant traffic. But there was one thing out here I could never get enough of. Sun.

I flew, and I flew fast through the soundstages and I quickly found one of their sets, the interior of a police station, the detectives' room with cramped desks and one of them with a name plate that said "Melissa Lee." The lights were off and it was nearly pitch black, but that doesn't matter to a ghost.

I had been on set with Sun before. We met when she was in an orange juice commercial and I was working on the crew. But I had never been on the set of her TV show, never seen her working since she hit it big.

I sat in the chair behind her beat-up metal desk and looked slowly around the room. I had seen every episode of her show. I had found a man in Tucson that watched it religiously, even the reruns, and would show up there on Thursday nights and watch it with him.

So I knew this room well. The whiteboard they were always putting pictures of their suspects on and drawing theories. The narrow table with the coffeepot and refrigerator below it where they would have crucial conversations to move the plot forward. The stained beige walls that looked like they hadn't been painted in decades. The grubby linoleum floor where Melissa Lee nearly bled out the time the gang took over the precinct.

But my view now was of a room without a roof and with only three sides. The illusion of this being a real room with real detectives was quickly eroding. I mean, I used to work in rooms like this, I know how the Hollywood sausage is made. I know the realities of making illusions seem real. And still it bothered me.

Of course, I saw Sun every time I saw Melissa Lee, but after seven seasons, the character was a different person in my mind than the actress.

When I flew down here, I had thought it would be fun to see Sun work, but I turned to go, no longer wanting to erode any more of my illusions. I didn't want to follow the lead to my murderer, which involved someone close to me, and I didn't want to see Sun dressed like Melissa Lee and out of character.

I had shattered enough illusions lately. I needed a break.

I got up and walked out of the set and saw the new ghost, Darla, standing in front of a director's chair.

She had a sheepish look on her face, her red lips pursed. She held out her hand. "I'm sorry I was such an ass over there," she said, nodding towards the other sound-stage. "I'm new to this and… well… I was just intimidated. You're *the* Walter Anchor."

Now there's some irony for you. I appear to be more famous as a ghost detective than I was as an actor. "Not a problem," I said, trying to put on my best boyish grin. "This is your case."

"I'm not good at apologies," she said, "but I could sure use a hand."

I smiled and nodded. A distraction was just what I needed and I really didn't care much what it was.

Chapter Six

DARLA ASSIGNED ME CORPSE DUTY. I WAS USED TO running the show and this was the kind of thing I would hand off to one of Anchor's Irregulars, like Blinky or Fredrick. I would let them tag along and learn from the medical examiner and then come report to me.

After we flew out of the soundstage and were hovering above the one that Emily popped us to, Darla pointed below to the paramedics wheeling the body to the ambulance. "You stick with the stiff, like you said. Okay? Darla will follow the hoity-toity actress."

I just stared at her.

"Please," she added and smiled. She looked a lot nicer when she smiled.

I nodded. If Emily was here, she'd laugh at me and say this was "bassackwards." But when I had been working in Hollywood, I had spent a lot more time behind the camera than in front of it, so it was no big deal. Maybe Emily was right, and this was what I needed. To be doing something useful, but maybe it would be better to do it here in Hollywood and to have less responsibility.

"Sure," I said with a smile I actually meant. "This is your case, Darla. I'm happy to help."

She was taking a deep breath to argue with me and then her eyes got wide. "Really?" she asked.

I shrugged. "Yeah. Really. I bet you could teach me a thing or two."

She blinked and then stared at me hard, her blue eyes drilling into me. Maybe I had laid it on too thick.

"It's been a bad few weeks," I said with a sigh. "I welcome the distraction."

She smiled and nodded knowingly, and I flew down just in time to go in the ambulance with the corpse. Not much to see, he was zipped into a black body bag. The two paramedics, both young men, looked bored and chatted about fantasy football as the ambulance driver headed us toward the morgue.

Ghosts have shuffled off their biology and that changes a lot of things. No need for food or water or a bathroom break, and that can make you really patient. Except you know how your mind can just go crazy sometimes? Well, as a ghost you don't have any of that biology to interrupt your mind, so it can go really crazy.

The dead are great at physical patience, but not necessarily mental patience.

Which is to say, I didn't pay much attention to what was going on. I hovered just inside the roof of the ambulance, my mind spinning away.

About my past and my potential murderer. After I died, I discovered that my long-time dental assistant Mary Paulson had a huge crush on me. She also had a struggling marriage and a new baby and was devastated by my death. She, or her husband, had motive. Mary could have done it to try to preserve her marriage and her new family. Her husband could have done it in a fit of jealousy.

Not pretty, but the motivations for murder are never pretty.

That was the lead I couldn't bear to follow. And it was embarrassing in many ways, because even with my excellent ghostly memory, I had blocked it out and focused on the odd goings on at the office which led to my first case but had nothing to do with my murder.

I had loved Mary, but like a friend. I had relied on her every day at work. I just couldn't bear the thought of her being a part of my death. I couldn't handle the reality of my life being even less than I thought it was.

It's not only Hollywood that manufactures the illusions we consume.

And then there was Emily and the friction between us because I hadn't shared this with her. So much so, that she had thought I was pining for my Hollywood life and hunted for a murder out here for me to investigate.

My mind raced as the ambulance navigated the busy streets of LA and got us to the morgue where the body was unloaded, wheeled in, and transferred to a stainless-steel table.

I wasn't doing a very good job for Darla. I should have been listening carefully. You never know how these mysteries are going to twist on you—but the good ones usually do.

Once in the morgue, I remembered the actor's name. It was Edward Lincoln. He had also been on *The Wild and the Willing* for a few decades. I didn't watch the show, but I don't think this was the first time his character had died on it, but it definitely would be the last.

The morgue was pretty standard, in the basement of the building, short windows at the tops of the wall letting in some natural light. There was the obligatory wall of stainless-steel doors that held refrigerated corpses, two stainless-steel tables, sinks, and cabinets full of medical equipment.

After an hour, a young man with freckles and curly reddish-brown hair came in. He had "Dr. Tomas" embroidered on his white lab coat.

Okay, time for the autopsy, this was going to get good now. But that is not what happened. He undressed the body, examined it, drew some blood, shoved a thermometer in Lincoln's liver to gauge the time of death, and shoved him into one of the drawers.

With a yawn and a glance at his watch, he closed up the morgue and left, taking the blood with him.

It was late afternoon. I doubted that murder was even suspected. Nothing was going to happen until the morning, but I couldn't be sure of that. I had to stay here, watch the body, and stew in my own dilemma overnight.

That's a lot of dilemma stewing. I groaned and regretted agreeing to help Darla. She sure hadn't done me any favors by putting me on morgue duty.

And, yes, I had done that many times with Anchor's Irregulars, the ghosts that help us out with cases back in Tucson. A ghost who goes by Blinky often did it. He claimed to love it, but as I experienced it, I had to wonder if he really did. Maybe I should mix things up more with the team.

But I didn't have a team. I was alone working with a new strange ghost with nothing to do but stew.

So that's what I did.

Chapter Seven

THE HOURS SLOWLY TICKED AWAY AS THE SUN SET outside and I just paced the linoleum floor of the morgue.

My choice was to hang out in an empty morgue or…

Or what?

I could leave and go try to find Emily. It would take me a few hours to fly back to Tucson, but that sounded a whole lot more pleasant than my other choice.

Except I'm not built that way. It's probably why I've turned out to be a decent detective. Mysteries seem to infect me, like a virus, and I just have to know.

Even if I couldn't write my stories and get the authorities the facts they need to make arrests, I think I would still do it.

When I was alive, I finished plenty of mediocre books just because I had to know what the ending was. The same goes for TV shows. I get hooked and I can't step away.

It's like the external puzzle gets internalized and I'm incomplete until it is solved. If the mystery, once it infects me, is like a virus, drilling into my cells and changing me, then solving the mystery is the only cure, the only way to make me better.

And, yes, I am the guy that was addicted to gambling and propofol when I was alive, and now I am addicted to solving mysteries. My body is gone, but much remains the same.

I paced the bland off-white floor of the morgue pondering all of this.

Morning takes a long time to get here for a ghost alone in a morgue. After an hour of pacing, I was wishing that Edward Lincoln had some unfinished business and his soul would separate from his body and his ghost could tell me how he died.

If he knew, that is. Take it from me, just because you are a ghost, it doesn't mean you know how it all ended.

After another hour, I poked my head in all the corpse drawers and found a young man and an old woman. I was soon wishing either one of them would have ghosts attached. While dealing with brand-new ghosts is rarely easy and never fun, I was that bored.

After another hour, my mind fell back to wondering about Mary Paulson and her husband. About what happened my last night alive during the bits of it I can't remember because of the propofol I was overdosed with.

After the sun set and the city started to quiet, I began to doubt myself more and more. Despite Emily's insistence that I was murdered, what if it had just been an accidental overdose? What if I had done this to myself?

I've built my afterlife on the idea that I was murdered. If I wasn't… well, that's the kind of thing that can send a ghost careening toward the bardo.

And as I contemplated it, as I paced in the dark morgue, I finally understood why I hadn't told Emily about it. Telling her would lead us to investigate Mary and her husband. This long past my death, it would be hard to find anything, but ghosts can be patient.

The result of the investigation, which would likely take a long time, months even, would be one of three things.

If Mary killed me, it would be a betrayal of someone close to me, someone I cared about.

If it was her jealous husband, then that would kinda be on me for not seeing how Mary felt, not dealing with it appropriately, and not being a good friend to Mary who had confided in me how her and her husband fought. How he sometimes hit her.

And if we found nothing, then the only logical conclusion would be that I had done this to myself.

As I paced, I discarded the jealous husband theory. He would have to know about propofol and how to administer an injection. He was a former soldier and a construction worker, so that made no sense.

That left either Mary did it or I did it, and neither was acceptable.

I know, I know, you're probably thinking, "Suck it up, Walter. Face the reality and deal with it." Well... maybe you are not saying it to me, but as I type this, I am yelling it at my past self. At the top of my non-existent lungs.

Except I couldn't face it. Even though I'm dead, I'm still human, and there are just some things I can't deal with.

All of this is to say that it was a very long night, and when in the morning a middle-aged woman walked in the door, I was never so happy in my life to witness an autopsy.

UNLIKE A WELL-DONE TV SHOW, THE DAY-TO-DAY LIFE of a medical examiner involves a lot of paperwork, a lot of safety protocols when you are dealing with human tissue, and a lot of slow, methodical work.

That's why they always cut to the scene where the intelligent but quirky medical examiner delivers just the facts needed to the diligent detectives.

But for me, after the night I had had, I was happy for the paperwork and the slow prep and the safety measures. But I'll do you the favor of cutting to the crucial bits.

Dr. Prescott was a thin woman approaching sixty, with long black hair streaked with grey pulled into a ponytail, dressed in pale pink scrubs and a white lab coat. She was methodical, but efficient, pulling more tissues samples early on and sending them off to the lab.

She was assisted by a short young woman with dark skin named Alison who appeared to be quite nervous through it all while she followed instructions, took notes, and helped pull Edward Lincoln apart a piece at a time.

I watched them moving the body from the drawer onto a table. Examining his skin for wounds. And then sawing through his sternum and exposing his organs.

Yeah, Edward Lincoln had died for the last time on *The Wild and the Willing*. A bone-saw ripping you open is an undeniable curtain call.

And while I won't give you all of the details, I loved it. I took a gross anatomy class in dental school where we carved up a smelly cadaver over the course of a semester, but this was something else entirely. It was fresh, it was fast, it was real.

Kind of made me wish I had gone to medical school, but that would have taken even longer than becoming a dentist.

So, Edward Lincoln did have what Prescott termed a "cardiac event" as I first guessed with Emily. He also had two stints and fairly clogged arteries. Not to mention his greying liver, and the damage to his lungs from decades of smoking.

Lincoln may have looked good on the outside, but he was in terrible shape under the hood.

The heart, though, was fascinating. The decaying heart had a grey section on the dark red from a previous myocardial infarction, a heart attack. But that is not what killed him, according to Dr. Prescott.

There were two wires in his heart, one that went to the right atrium and the other to the right ventricle. The tiny wires led through a vein to a roundish metal disk about an inch and a half across that had been implanted under his skin. A pacemaker.

She pulled it out and rinsed it off and showed it to her assistant, Alison.

"I'll bet you lunch that this did it," she said, a grim smile playing on her thin lips.

"How do you know?" Alison asked.

"He had this thing because his heart didn't always know how to beat right. Beyond the cholesterol blocking his arteries, he had electrical problems with his heart. If this stopped working, his heart rate could plummet and he would just pass out and…"

"Look like he was sleeping," Alison finished.

"Right. And he was an actor acting like a corpse when this happened. No one would have noticed."

"But…" Alison began, her gloved hands touching the device, "wouldn't that be a rare event? The batteries shouldn't just fail."

Prescott smiled a quirky smile that lit up her hazel eyes. "So is it a bet?"

Alison shook her head and smiled.

Chapter Eight

So here is something I didn't know, but modern pacemakers can be accessed and adjusted wirelessly just like hearing aids.

There are security protocols and the equipment to do it is regulated, but maybe someone just turned off Edward Lincoln's heart while he lay there in that casket. Maybe someone murdered him via remote control.

This mystery was now in my blood, in my cells (even though I possessed neither). It was part of me. I had to see it through. I had to know if that was it and who did it.

In most cases, the murderer was someone close to the victim and I wasn't part of that, being stuck here with the dead guy. It was starting to itch at me like a mosquito bite. I wanted to investigate his life, find out if he was married, had any lovers on the side, a psychotic ex-wife or two, or disgruntled children. One of them that was technically inclined.

While my mind churned with all these details, Dr. Prescott called for a CSI technician and they got back to the autopsy, but I wasn't that interested in the details anymore. I knew how Edward Lincoln died, and I knew he was murdered.

I watched, just in case something else relevant came up, but I really needed Darla to come by, to check in and find out what I know, to take me to the frontlines of this case that had infected me so.

THE WHEELS MOVE SLOWLY IN A BUREAUCRACY, AND after the autopsy was finished, I stuck with Dr. Prescott as she drafted the report, went to lunch at a nearby restaurant with Alison, and then did another autopsy and drafted another report.

No technician came to look at the pacemaker. No diligent detectives came by to check on the results. No Darla. No other ghosts. And I found myself alone for another night in a dark morgue pacing over the plain industrial linoleum floor.

The truth is being a ghost detective in Hollywood isn't any more glamorous than being a ghost detective in Tucson. I can't interview witnesses. I can only follow and observe. It's slow, boring work. It can give you a lot of time to think, but I would usually have Emily with me and boredom was never a problem when she was in her four-year-old mode.

That night, I really missed her. I also came to grips with how dependent I had become on her. She had saved me. She had tutored me along as a ghost until I was functional. She had been with me for each murder I had been involved in solving.

And while it hurt, while part of me was angry at her for dumping me out here like this, I was also grateful for the clarity.

To put this night in perspective for the living, you know those nights when you lie awake and can't shut your mind off and it keeps going around and around but not getting anywhere? Well, that is just another night for a lot of ghosts.

It's why we gather at midnight at the graveyard and share stories or put on plays in the Midnight Circle. It's why we socialize a lot, because without it there is only your mind going in circles. And that night it was my mind spinning around all of this while I paced.

I thought of flying back to the graveyard for the Midnight Circle, but this case was so weird and had so infected me, I couldn't take the chance of missing something.

So I paced and I stewed and I paced and stewed some more. And then I couldn't stand doing that, so I started flying through the old building investigating every nook and cranny, every office, every lab, every storeroom.

And then I started flying around the outside of the building for some variety. Around and around, faster and faster. I don't have an inner ear anymore, so no issues with getting dizzy.

I swirled around the building under the sodium glow of the Los Angeles metro area, cars buzzing by on the I-5 all night long.

I made it a game. How fast could I go, how close could I come to the building without touching it. How sharply could I turn the corners.

A silly game, a childish game, but it was something to do. You living always have something to do because of your biology. It demands so much attention. The dead have to come up with other things to do.

The top of the building had steeply pitched roofs

coming together in an eight-sided construction that looked something like a bell tower.

This building clearly had history. It was made of red bricks and ornate, but not like a church. Maybe it was originally a courthouse or something. I was over five hundred laps around the building—yes, I was counting and, yes, I was that bored—when I saw a little girl with blond ringlets standing on the tiptop of the tower. She was a tad transparent dressed in blue shorts and a white T-shirt with a red lollipop print on it, her hands on her hips, her lips pressed tightly together.

"Emily!" I yelled, flying to her.

I landed on the curved roof of the tower down a bit from her so we were eye to eye.

She looked me up and down and did a tsk-tsk.

I looked and saw that my form was wispy, the ends of my trench coat diffuse, my ghostly form a lot more transparent than hers.

A ghost's appearance often reflects their mental/emotional state and I was a bit out of it. I took a deep ghostly breath and stared into Emily's green eyes and calmed myself like she taught me. Being dead, we don't actually breathe, but acting like we are alive has a physical analogue in the afterlife. So I calmed down. My form firmed up. My trench coat came into focus.

Flying, while it can be a lot of fun, is not something the living can do so it is not good afterlife hygiene. We don't have bodies to maintain, but our ghostly forms take focus.

"Better," she said with a nod and a smile. It hadn't taken me long. I wasn't the newbie ghost she had found haunting my former dental office manager in her bathroom anymore.

"This case is fascinating," I said, the words rushing out. "There's another ghost. Darla. She claimed the case and I

35

agreed to help out. I followed the dead guy, Edward Lincoln. They did the autopsy today. It's his pacemaker. I think someone turned it off and he died in that casket on the set. You were right, it is a murder. I'm so glad you are back. God, I really missed you, Emily. And I could really use your help finding Darla. She hasn't checked in on me. She knows about us, by the way. Read some of our cases while she was alive. I think it's why she's doing this. I…"

I finally stopped when I realized how long I had been babbling on and the frown on Emily's young, round face fully registered.

"What's wrong?" I asked. Something had to be wrong. This was the kind of weird case that Emily just lived for.

"I'm happy for you, Walter," she said, but her frown stayed in place.

My mind slipped for a moment trying to figure it out. This couldn't be the four-year-old Emily, she'd be excited about the gory details. This was the eighty-year-dead Emily watching her protégé excited about something after being so grumpy.

The color of the lollipop on her T-shirt changes color to reflect her mood. It's something of a mood ring and the lollipop had swirled into a deep, sad blue.

And then the picture clicked into place.

"I don't want to do this without you," I said.

Her smooth brow furrowed. "You don't?"

I shook my head. "No. I'm stuck here. I can't pop. I have no idea where Darla is. There's nothing to do and…"

Her eyes hardened and she crossed her arms in front of her, pursing her lips again, some angry red invading the blue of the lollipop.

I shook my head. My words were coming out too fast again. "It's you, Emily. I miss you. I miss doing this togeth- er," I said, trying to correct my mistake. I made it sound like I just needed her because I can't pop. "I miss your delight in the gory details. You would have loved this autopsy. You could actually see the damage on his heart from his previous myocardial infarction. And the liver… whew, I bet they could smell the alcohol. I…"

I looked away to the cars buzzing by on the highway. This wasn't what Emily needed to hear. I needed to treat her like my friend, like my teacher.

"I'm sorry I haven't told you what I found out when I wrote about my last day," I said. "I figured it out though, why I haven't said anything." There was a burger joint across the street, it must have been close to 2 a.m., but there were still cars lined up at the drive-through, the living needing to feed their biology and often not being choosy about what they shove in.

"I just can't face it, " I continued. "It's embarrassing, but I can't. It's more than I can handle. I want to tell you and I'm sure I'll tell you someday but…" I ended in a weak shrug, still not looking at my friend.

"Do you want to stay here?" she asked quietly.

I didn't know what level she was asking the question, but I guessed it wasn't just about this building, but this town. "This was never an easy town to live in," I said, looking back at her. "I mean, you were right, part of me loved it so much. It was my dream to be a working actor here. But now…? I think if I stayed here, I would end up haunting Sun and that wouldn't be fair to her."

It was true, I knew it was. I would fight it, hard, but I'd soon have a bad enough day and her house would be only a few minutes flight away and I would go there. I would see her and I would never want to leave. Sun would be my addiction, not gambling or propofol. I would lose myself again.

"But that is my old life," I said quietly. "You are my afterlife, Emily."

Emily nodded slowly, her eyes tearing up. There are some ghosts at the graveyard that are "romantic" and what I was professing here was not that kind of thing. Emily was my best dead friend. She was what made my afterlife worth living and I loved her.

But I didn't say any of that. I could feel my cheeks redden, echoing the actions of a biology long gone. And while I hadn't told her about Mary Paulson, at least I had told her why I wasn't telling her.

"Where's the stiff now?" she asked, a grin forming on her face, the lollipop on her T-shirt swirling into a happy red with bits of curious yellow. "You wanna show me and walk me through it?"

I nodded and smiled so big. Emily was back and I couldn't be happier. But that didn't mean this was going to be easy.

Chapter Nine

As soon as we got into the morgue and I pointed out the drawer that contained Edward Lincoln, Emily walked in. His corpse was covered in a sheet so we couldn't see the Frankenstein style stitching that held his chest together, but there was enough light leakage for her to see his face and hands and feet.

We stood there and I went over everything I knew. I told her about the autopsy in gruesome detail. I showed her the office where the pacemaker was sitting on the cheap wooden desk.

"Are you sure?" she asked, touching the roundish pacemaker with her ghostly finger. She couldn't actually touch it, of course. It's not at all easy for the dead to interact with the living, and even harder with inanimate objects.

"That's what Dr. Prescott said when she was explaining the device to her assistant," I said. "If they can be adjusted wirelessly, then it stands to reason that they can be turned off wirelessly."

Emily looked at me, her green eyes wide while she bit on her lip. "But... JJ did those things, he... Oh crap..."

She stared off into space for a moment and then grabbed my hand. "We have to go."

With a pop we were standing on top of a rock spire with the Grand Canyon all around us. The gibbous moon illuminated the formations and the layers of rock in ghostly shades of grey, like we were in the middle of a frothing sea at night made of rock. We were on top of one of the temples in the middle of the canyon, and we were not alone.

JJ Lynch was there staring off to the north. His form was firm, jeans and a long-sleeved black T-shirt, and he glowed with his own light. He was a ghost. The first ghost to use the SECI chamber and write about the afterlife. He turned, a smile on his boyishly handsome face.

"Emily. Walter," he said with a nod.

"Sorry to bother you, JJ," Emily said. "We are working on a case and have a quick question for you."

He smiled, but there was something a bit strained about it. I had heard that this was his retreat spot, where he came when he wanted to be alone. Maybe that reluctant smile was about that. "Ask away," he said.

Emily flapped her hand at me and said, "Tell him about the thingy and the remote control part that could... you know."

"The pacemaker?" I asked.

She nodded. "Tell him how it works."

"Okay..." I said, not quite sure where this was going. "It monitors your heart rate and when it gets too low, it kind of substitutes your body's own electrical signals to keep it beating. Modern pacemakers can be adjusted wirelessly."

Emily nodded, her curls bouncing. "How hard would it be for a ghost to fry one of those?"

I stood there blinking, my mind catching up to the leap

Emily had made. Maybe it wasn't shut off wirelessly, maybe a ghost did it. And if a ghost could do that… well, I didn't want to finish that thought.

"For me?" JJ asked with a grim smile.

Emily nodded.

"Not hard if the person wasn't moving," he said. "But if you've never messed with electricity?" He shrugged. "Well, that would take some doing."

When JJ was a new ghost haunting those responsible for his death, he had learned how to turn light switches on and off. He had eventually done a lot more than that. He knew more about manipulating electricity than any other ghost I had heard of.

"Thank you," Emily said. "I'm sorry to have disturbed you here."

"No problem," he said with a grin. "I hope you solve the case."

She took my hand, and my mind still reeling, she popped us back to the morgue's office. She pointed at the pacemaker. "So our suspect list just got a lot bigger. A whole lot bigger."

Chapter Ten

EMILY POPPED US TO DARLA. IT WAS THE NEXT MOVE. And now that I think back on it, it's a wonder how easily Emily and I just got back into the rhythm of things. Maybe her dumping me here had been a test. Maybe she had been desperate to shake me out of my depression. Maybe I don't fully understand the complexity of my best ghost friend who died when she was four but has existed for over eighty years as a ghost.

The last part is undoubtedly true, but what was clear is that Emily and Walter were back. The case had infected us both and we just had to know.

And yes, I can see that this "infection" I've been talking about sounds a lot like what happens when you shoot up with propofol or when a gambling addict sits down to a game of Texas Hold'em. And you could even say we were addicted to solving murders.

I will admit that there is clearly something in it for us, but unlike propofol and gambling (or alcohol or meth) we were doing something useful. We were bringing criminals to justice. We were adding to society, not taking away.

That is what makes it different than those other addictions.

And, yes, we were enjoying it.

So, Emily popped us to Darla.

But it wasn't what we expected.

Actually, given the woman I had met briefly, I didn't know what to expect, but this wasn't it.

She was immersed in a large, bubbling hot tub with Sheila Green, the actress that had been playing the grieving wife to her husband played by Edward Lincoln on *The Wild and the Willing*.

Shelia was nude, a glass of champagne in her hand, tears running down her face and her mascara running.

Darla was in the water next to her, her large ghostly form also looking nude as she drank and cried and carried on right next to Shelia Green.

My jaw hung open. I had never seen a naked ghost before, but I guess it could make sense. I appear to be wearing a long trench coat and a fedora because I practiced that after Emily and I solved our first murder—she thought it was befitting of the role. But before that, I had been in blue scrubs because that is what I identified with.

Maybe Darla had been a nudist. Maybe this was her default form.

It didn't really matter, though, it was just surprising. As was the crying and the drinking of faux champagne. Ghosts can't drink and the champagne glass had to be an extension of her ghostly form.

"I loved the narcissistic bastard," Shelia said, her voice slurred. The hot tub was in a lovely courtyard surrounded by tall trees and well-tended gardens. "To Eddie, my Eddie, the only Eddie I ever loved." She took a sip, tilting the glass too far and pouring champagne over her chest and she giggled.

"Darla loved the narcissistic bastard," Darla said, her voice matching that of Shelia Green. She took a sip from her glass, which now that I looked at it was empty. "To Eddie, my Eddie, the only Eddie Darla ever loved."

"Is that her?" Emily hissed, her chin jabbing out at Darla.

I nodded and sighed.

Shelia muttered more about Eddie and Darla copied it except this time I heard it differently. Darla was amplifying Shelia's tone, parodying it a little, almost like she was trying to reflect it back to the grieving woman.

"I don't think she knows what she's doing," Emily whispered.

"Darla heard that!" Darla said, rising up out of the water. She wasn't wet, of course, her red hair dry but wild around her, glasses still hanging around her neck by a chain.

I averted my gaze. No biology means that nudity doesn't hold a charge anymore, but it was just the way I was raised.

Darla floated out of the pool and stood in front of us. I stared at her bare feet on the courtyard's flagstone, her nails painted a bright red.

"Hi, I'm Emily," Emily said, extending her hand to Darla, "and I died in 1931 of dysentery."

"Darla knows who you are," she said, "and Darla will not be fooled by your cutesy appearance. Darla knows those adorable curls hide a wicked old woman."

In the hot tub, Shelia kept babbling on about Eddie and how much she loved him and how much she hated him, interspersed with drunken laughter and splashing.

I could feel Emily's mood change. Her lollipop edged into the dangerous spectrum of red and I saw her throw her shoulders back and straighten her spine. "Walter here has some interesting updates for you," Emily said, all business. "And we were wondering what you found in your investigation."

"Something wrong there, Mr. Anchor?" Darla asked me. "You got a problem with what a real woman looks like? Did you never find yourself in the presence of a goddess, or did you only spend your time with too-skinny-to-be-healthy actresses?"

Now she was making me mad and I was beginning to wonder if Darla had multiple personalities. The brash and insulting Darla I had first met that always spoke of herself in the third person, and the reasonable Darla that had asked for my help.

I raised my head and met her blue eyes. "Emily and I are going to leave now. When you find yourself wishing to have a civil discussion, we'll be on the roof of the Los Angeles County Morgue. I trust you know where that is."

I gave Darla my best smile and took Emily's hand.

"Darla doesn't need you two to solve this murder. Darla has it figured out, you know. So many suspects. So much motive and opportunity. You two will be sitting there waiting for Darla for a very long time. Darla is just fine without—"

Emily popped us away and I was very grateful.

Chapter Eleven

EMILY DID POP US BACK TO THE MORGUE, BUT WE DIDN'T stay long. It was still dark and nothing would be happening here until morning. After we had given a reasonable amount of time for Darla to get sane and fly over here, she popped us back to the soundstage on the Warner Brothers lot where Edward Lincoln had died.

The main lights were all off, but there was still enough light for us to see. The set was blocked with yellow police tape but otherwise it was untouched. The cameras were halfway moved to do the close-ups, cables snaking over the floor, some of them not hooked up yet. The casket was open in the middle of it all with the faux funeral home walls behind it with unlit stained glass that looked eerie in the darkness.

"What do you know about him?" Emily asked, nodding toward the casket.

I shrugged. I mean, it was a reasonable question, I used to be an actor, and even after I stopped, I worked in Holly-wood for a while and paid attention. "He was in his late sixties and had been on this show for over twenty years. He had been married and divorced three times, had four kids along the way. I had heard rumors he could be kinda grabby."

Emily started pacing back and forth in front of the ornate casket. We weren't here because we expected to find anything, we were here for a change of scenery that might help us think of something that would get us closer to solving this one.

She stopped and looked at me. "I guess we should start with the wives and then move on to the children."

I nodded.

"So," Emily began. "First wife. What was her name? What did she look like?"

If I had still been alive, I wouldn't have been able to tell you, but somehow our memories get better without all the flesh. I had absorbed a ton of Hollywood trivia that I could recall easily now that I was dead.

"Helen Lincoln," I said. "Former model with green eyes and long black hair. Played a Bond girl once and didn't act much after that. She had two children with Edward and they were married for eight years. They've been divorced for thirty-one years."

Emily took my hand and her face constricted in concentration. Emily was good at popping, but this was asking a lot. I summoned Helen Lincoln into my mind, visualized her as strongly as I could, but my memories of her appearance were from several decades ago.

It took a minute, but with a pop, we were gone.

Hellen Lincoln was living in New York City and

was up for a sunrise breakfast. She was an elegant sixty-something with a few more pounds and wrinkles than her early days, but her black hair was still long and luxurious and her blue eyes were sharp and clear.

She had a corner apartment with floor-to-ceiling windows overlooking Central Park. She was alone dressed in a dark blue robe drinking coffee, eating papaya, and reading the paper.

"Does she look like a remote-control murderer?" I asked once we had searched the apartment—which was all high ceilings and abstract artwork and Zen elegance—and found nothing of interest.

Emily shrugged and stared as Hellen dug into the soft yellow/orange flesh of the papaya and took a delicate bite.

I so miss eating. The feel of a piece of steak in my mouth as I bite down, saliva flowing, the stomach grumbling happily. The simplest of things, the most basic thing, and yet so precious when you don't have it anymore.

The newspaper rattled as Hellen changed the page and took a quiet sip of coffee. She was calm and relaxed. She wasn't acting like the father of her children had just died, so either she didn't know or she was a psychopath and quite capable of murder.

"We have to stay, don't we?" I asked Emily.

She turned and smiled at me. "You have to stay, Walter. Tell me about the second wife and I'll go visit her."

I sighed and told her about Melany Tabor, who had been a director on *The Wild and the Willing* during Lincoln's early years there. She was a brunette with generous curves and a scar on her chin.

Emily popped away and I was left watching Hellen Lincoln eat breakfast while the sun rose over Central Park.

I had been to New York once, for a dental convention. I caught a show on Broadway and really enjoyed that, but I can't say that I understood the city. It was so dense, so many people when I was used to the urban sprawl of California and Arizona.

After breakfast, she took a shower so I wandered the sparsely furnished apartment and looked at all the family photos, a few of them featuring a young Edward Lincoln, many of them featuring their two children, a boy and a girl, now grown with children of their own. They were both tall with black hair like their parents and it looked like one of their grandchildren had recently gotten married.

This wasn't that big of a family, but if we had to follow each of them until we saw something that let us know if they were or weren't involved, this could take forever. We would need help.

There was something odd about the apartment. The generic artwork. The sparse furnishing. The single bedroom. The family pictures in frames on the furniture, none of them hanging on the wall. And then I remembered that I had read in *Variety* that Hellen liked doing a show on Broadway every few years.

That nearly ruled her out. She would have had to have flown to LA, somehow got the equipment to turn Edward Lincoln's heart off, and flown back without being noticed. On top of that, she would have had to know enough about the shooting schedule of Edward's soap opera to know when the funeral scene was being shot.

Not likely. Not likely at all.

I heard crying from the bedroom and found Hellen balled up on the floor slumped against her bed, a pale green towel wrapped around her wet body. She was staring at her phone, a text message that read, "Sorry to tell you this, doll, but Eddie is gone. Died on set like the bastard would have wanted."

There are lots of ways that people cry. The way they

cry in public is way different than the way they cry in private. Hellen didn't know I was there so what I was seeing wasn't a show. Her weeping was controlled but intense, tears running down her cheeks, but she wasn't making that much noise.

She clicked on the link that came with the text that sent her to some cheesy entertainment site and a silly article that had a picture of the set with the yellow police tape and another picture of Shelia Green talking to the police with tears running down her cheeks.

The article talked about Edward Lincoln, his acting career, his three wives and four children, his long stint on *The Wild and the Willing*. It was a simple article likely compiled from Lincoln's Wikipedia page. Just crappy click-bait designed to foist a few ads on the reader.

Hellen's demeanor changed when she saw Shelia Green. Her nostrils flared and her lips pursed. "Bitch," she said under her breath.

I stayed with her while she googled and cried and looked at old pictures of the two of them that she found on the internet. She did this for about half an hour before she shakily rose to her feet, put the phone down on the bedstand, and went back into the bathroom.

She was grieving her long-divorced husband and the father of her children. Add that to her being in New York and I didn't think she did it.

I gave her privacy and went back into the living room and watched Central Park wake up and wondered how my ex-wife Sun reacted when she got the news of my death, when they told her it was a suicide and that I had over-dosed on propofol.

Seeing Hellen Lincoln like that stirred something in me. I wasn't quite ready to go there, but I knew I would have to follow the clue I had to my own murder.

A death is never isolated, it affects those that love us. Maybe I wouldn't like the truth once I found it, but it would have the virtue of at least being the truth.

Chapter Twelve

"MELANY TABOR IS A BUST," EMILY SAID WHEN SHE popped back to me. Helen Lincoln was still in her bedroom and I was still watching New York wake up and pondering my own death and how it affected those that loved me.

While I waited, I stood here and stared at Central Park enough that I thought I almost understood New York City, at least a little bit. You had the tall buildings crowding it on all sides, full of people and their problems and their drama, but in the park, you had grass and trees and water and nature.

It was controlled and a bit contrived, but it was abundant nature and very accessible to people living on this island. So you could enjoy the people and the city and all the many activities, but you could easily escape if you wanted and be reminded of nature, smell fresh air, gaze at the water, walk for miles.

Arizona was full of open land, and cities like Tucson had some excellent parks, but the sprawl and the heat kept people away. How many people lived within a twenty-minute walk of Central Park? You couldn't match that in any western city.

Emily was standing quietly next to me staring at the park. Maybe sensing my mood. Maybe just enjoying the view.

She had dumped me in Hollywood and that had woken me up some, and now I had to wonder what it would be like to be a ghost in New York City. How many ghosts does a city like this have? And there must be plenty of murders to investigate, that's for sure.

I took a deep ghostly breath and softened my sense of vision as I looked at the tiny people below in the park. Not having eyes, it was different than you might think, but what I was trying to do was the equivalent of focusing on my peripheral vision.

I didn't focus on individual figures far below but on all of them that I could see moving in the park. Runners. Bikers. Walkers. The homeless starting their day.

And then I saw it. Some of them weren't moving quite normally. Some of them seemed a little brighter and a little bit transparent. A lot of them. Actually, most of them.

"Ghosts," I whispered. "There are so many ghosts."

The thought was both exciting and terrifying. So many dead. So much unfinished business. So many suffering in the bardo or haunting their loved ones or those they blamed for their deaths.

"Oh, yeah," Emily said. "City's like this, they're just rotten with ghosts."

"Where do they all go?" I asked. In Tucson we mostly called the graveyard home, but here? In a city this big and this old. Just do the math, there could be thousands and thousands of ghosts.

It made my experience in Tucson seem quaint.

"Everywhere," Emily said with a shrug. "There are

tons at the graveyards, lots on the roofs, others here and there. Not that different, just more in a smaller space. Same as the living."

I shook my head, shaking off the thought. Something to contemplate, but we had a strange murder to solve. I turned to Emily and focused on her, letting my view of the ghost-filled Central Park go.

"What did you find?" I asked.

Emily's face twisted into a sour configuration as if she had just bit into a lemon. "Alzheimer's. She's in a facility. Not pretty."

I stared at her, not sure what to say, my head still full of thoughts of the New York ghost population. Before I could come up with something, she asked, "What about this one?"

I shook my head. "She just found out and is grieving. For real."

Emily pursed her lips and nodded. "Third wife?"

"Amanda York," I said, staring back out at the city, my eyes now easily finding the ghosts, a few flying from a high-rise apartment down toward the park like they had just woken up and were going for their morning flight around the hood. "She was thirty-one years younger than him. Rumor has it she was pregnant when they got married, but the marriage only lasted a year or so. She was his assistant and that's how they met. I only read about it, so I'm not sure what she looks like."

Emily crossed her arms and sighed dramatically, her cheeks puffing out and her lips flapping briefly. "That's not enough."

We stood in silence watching the sun brighten the trees below, the pedestrians looking like ants and the cars like toys, the ghosts interspersed among the living.

"The kids?" I asked Emily. "We've got pictures here of them."

Emily shrugged, her eyes distant. I couldn't tell if she was watching the scene below or somewhere else completely. But I had to agree with her indifference. This didn't feel like a kid thing, much more like a wife thing or a lover thing.

But we didn't have a way to find Amanda York and we had no idea where Edward Lincoln had lived, so we couldn't search for clues there. It's not like we can google it.

And then something tickled in my mind. I had missed something. Something obvious.

Helen had called Shelia a bitch. Shelia had been truly grieving when she was alone in the hot tub with Darla. "Shelia Green and Edward Lincoln were together," I said.

"Really?" Emily asked. She's not good at these kinds of things, having never experienced the full power of hormones while alive.

"There had been rumors over the years," I said, "that Lincoln cheated on his wives a lot and with her specifically and repeatedly. That she was the reason his marriage with Helen ended. But he wasn't married when he died, hadn't been for a few years. I was wrong about Shelia's reaction on the set, there was something genuine there."

Emily was staring at me, her eyes wide. While she didn't understand these hormone driven things, she was fascinated by them. "Does that give her a motive?"

"Maybe," I said. "If he was cheating on her, but…"

"But what?" Emily asked, her voice eager.

"She seemed destroyed in the hot tub. There's something else… I just can't quite get it. Something we're missing."

Emily just stared at me as I racked my brain. Well, not my brain, specifically. I didn't have any grey matter, but you get my meaning. My mind, however, it was possible that I had one, worked much like it had worked with all that grey matter. I had a better memory but the mysteries of the subconscious seemed to survive death fully intact.

"Can you pop us to Shelia Green?" I asked. "Let's see what she's doing."

"But that… woman," Emily spat out, undoubtedly referring to Darla who was in the hot tub with Shelia Green last time we saw her.

"We won't stay long if she's there," I said.

Emily nodded and grabbed my arm, and with a "pop" we were gone.

Chapter Thirteen

WE FOUND SHELIA GREEN NAKED AND UNCONSCIOUS IN
bed on top of her satin green comforter in her spacious
bedroom, a nearly empty bottle of vodka and a spilled
bottle of sleeping pills on the bedstand beside her.

I rushed to her and leaned my head down to her chest
and could hear her heartbeat, but it was slow, maybe forty
beats per minute. She was bradycardic. She was dying.

The bedroom was large, with plush carpet, a big TV
hanging on the wall, a beautiful antique armoire, and a
chaise lounge. Expensive knickknacks were placed with
care, like a green oriental vase and a marble sculpture of a
reclining woman. Decorating the walls were elegantly
framed posters from Shelia's career, some of the movies
and plays she had been in. In other words, it was just what
I would have expected from a diva like Shelia Green.

Darla was there, her arms crossed as she stared at the
unconscious woman. She was back in her blue business
suit, a sneer on her face.

"She's dying," I shouted.

Darla just smiled.

I ignored the red-haired woman, grabbed Emily's hand, and flew us out of the house.

"What are we doing, Walter?" she asked.

"Getting the address," I said. "It's 911 time."

Shelia Green's house was up in the Hollywood hills. Not a big place, but gated and lovely. We got the address, Emily popped us to the hidden SECI chamber that I and a few other ghosts used. And I typed and typed fast.

"911. Shelia Green has overdosed in her home and needs immediate medical attention."

And then I left her address.

"911" is not the actual code, it's longer than that. After the first time I wrote about the code, every ghost that died after reading that story was using it when they made it to the SECI chamber. They all wanted to get a message to their loved ones right away. And all those 911s were waking up Tamara Watson, the woman that runs Afterlife Communications. She wasn't getting any sleep, so the code is no longer 911, and there is a system in place so she's not always the one fielding them.

So all of you thinking of 911ing your SECI communications after you die. Don't. It won't work. I'm also not going to say one thing about this hidden SECI chamber either. If the word ever got out, I would never be able to get these cases written up.

Emily popped us back to Shelia Green and we did what we could until the ambulance arrived.

If you read my first case, about Haley, you know what a dedicated ghost can do to hurt the living. You know what Haley and I did to her murderer. Well, there is a much less dramatic way a ghost can help the living. It's called, quite simply, "the warmth."

I can't say that I understand it, but ghosts can tap into a benevolent source of energy and channel it into the living. It's called "the warmth" because that is what it feels like. And, yes, warmth is a rare kind of sensation for a ghost, so if you feel it then you know when you are doing it right.

And that can be tricky because it is a subtle skill. Like much about being a ghost, it is about intent, but after that it is all about letting go. Not forcing it. Detaching.

Emily and I didn't talk, we walked into the bed, put our hands on Shelia Green, and let the warmth flow.

Darla glowered at us from next to the chaise lounge but didn't say anything.

"It's helping," I said after a few minutes when I could hear Shelia's heart rate increase just a touch. She was pale and her breathing was still very shallow, but it looked like we might be able to save her.

And that made all of this Hollywood madness worth it. Sure Shelia Green was a diva and was far too fond of herself, but she was a good actress and years ago when we had worked on that play, I had seen her be genuinely kind and I knew she did a lot for animal welfare charities.

And on a personal level, I didn't want the world thinking she had died of a suicide, just like the world thought I had. Not that many people had noticed my death.

But none of that really mattered, either. Emily and I were helping her because it was the right thing to do. Sure, I know without a doubt that there is an afterlife, but that doesn't make life any less precious or any less worth preserving.

"Darla doesn't like that you are doing that," Darla said, taking a step towards us, her face stuck in a deep frown, her eyes narrow. I had to wonder if we had found yet another one of her personalities.

But I was with the warmth and that wondering wasn't

something I was serious about, so I just let it go. And then the tickling in my mind that I was missing something came back.

Darla took another step toward us, the edges of her form starting to flicker red. Emily has her lollipop T-shirt that quite artfully reflects her mood, but a ghost experiencing extreme emotion and not in complete control of their form will sometimes have a visible aura around their form. Darla's was red. She was furious.

But why? I was missing something about Darla.

She had been so strange, so different, every time we met.

The big woman took another step toward us.

"I got this," Emily growled, stepping away from Shelia, and I heard her heart slow down again.

Emily had way more experience at this than I did. She was a much more capable ghost. I didn't want to leave the warmth, but I wasn't the one that Shelia needed.

"Stay, Emily," I said. "Please. You are better at this. I'll deal with Darla."

Emily gave me a worried nod and stepped back in as I stepped out, my relaxed mind suddenly seeing what I had missed.

The article that Helen Lincoln had read listed all of Edward Lincoln's ex-wives. The article said, "…had been married three times to Helen R. Lincoln, Melany A. Taylor, and Amanda D. York."

It had used middle initials.

Amanda D. York.

I remembered back in the morgue when Emily had been worried that a ghost might have done this. I remembered Darla telling us how much she read, that she had read about Emily and me, and she must have read about JJ and what he did with electricity.

60

Amanda Darla York.

Sheila Green had been the reason for Edward and Darla's divorce. Darla had killed Edward, had shorted out his pacemaker while he was in that casket for that shoot. He had passed out. No one had noticed and he had died.

The murderer was a ghost.

Darla had been in the hot tub amplifying Shelia's grief to drive her to this point, to this overdose.

"You know," I said as I stepped toward Darla and extended my hand, "we never met properly. Let's start over. My name is Walter Anchor and I died when someone overdosed me with propofol."

I was at the end of the bed, a furious Darla in front of me. The edges of her ghostly form were a bright, flickering red, her long red hair starting to form around her like she was in the presence of a massive amount of static electricity.

"Get out of my way," she said, her tone low and dangerous.

"Let me try for you," I said. "Your name is Amanda Darla York, and you died... let me guess, you died of a broken heart after Edward went back to Shelia, leaving you with his baby."

Darla's blue eyes found mine and beneath the fury there was pain. Her jaw moved as if she was struggling to find words and then she spoke. "Look at me," she said, slapping her chest. "Darla is not the kind of woman he wanted, or you for that matter. You want your Hollywood girls and not a real woman with a real body and a real heart."

That hurt because she was kinda right. Sun was the only woman for me. I hadn't even noticed Mary Paulson's quite obvious interest in me because she wasn't Sun and she didn't look like Sun.

But she was also wrong. Sun had plenty of heart and was plenty real. I will admit to some typical shallowness when it comes to the kind of packages I am attracted to. But heart always mattered to me. It wouldn't have worked with Sun if she hadn't had a heart and a mind to go along with her appearance.

Darla backed up a step, tears forming in her eyes, the red flickering around her ghostly forming dying down. "Eddie wasn't used to someone really caring for him, really loving him. We... we had our time, and it was... it was sweet." The tears were rolling down her cheeks. "But then he went back to that *woman*. While I was pregnant. With his child. I fought for him. So hard. I fought for our family, but he kept going bat to *her*. I—"

The red flared back to life and she charged, her face contorted in rage, her red hair swaying around her as if it had a life of its own, and she surged forward.

I didn't think. I braced myself and caught her and flew her up out of the house into the predawn LA sky.

Because of Emily, I know how to touch as a ghost. I know how to modulate my frequency to match another ghost's so we just don't go through each other. I hadn't had to think about it. I held her and flew straight up.

I was mad, her emotional state leaking into me through our contact. I was mad at myself for being so cowardly about facing all the facts of my own death. I was mad at the world for that accident that caused Sun's miscarriage and led to the crumbling of our marriage and my life with her. I was mad at myself for not making it in Hollywood, for letting my dreams go. And I was furious with myself for my retreat into addiction when I went back to Tucson and not getting proper help for it.

"Let me go!" Darla shouted.

I ignored her and flew straight up.

"Why the hell did you have me help, have me follow the body?" I asked.

She snorted. I could feel her struggling, feel her changing her frequency, but I kept matching mine to hers. "Darla knew the mighty Walter Anchor wouldn't let it go. Best to get him out of the way while Darla did what needed to be done."

That just made me laugh, because she was so wrong. I wouldn't have stayed, wouldn't have investigated but for her asking. I laughed because she had called me "mighty" when I couldn't even face the reality of my own death and find out the truth. I wasn't mighty. I was just trying to get by, to survive this afterlife, to do something worth doing while I'm here.

And with Darla up in the sky, I was doing what needed to be done, faking it and hoping it worked. I had no idea what to do with a murdering ghost that was intent on being a serial killer.

I know it's a very actorly thing, but I kind of think everyone should do a little improv. It was a fairly big part of my training as an actor and has served me well in this life… and afterlife. You take what you get, you improvise, you try to turn it into something good. You do it over and over until it starts to come naturally.

"Let Darla go!" she shouted. I could feel her rage intensifying and she was switching her frequency faster and faster, our forms going diffuse and then firming up. If this got much worse, I wouldn't be able to hold her.

And then she suddenly gave up and stopped struggling, but we weren't going up anymore, we started drifting down. She was trying to fly down while I was trying to fly up. I felt her wrap her big arms around me and she grunted with effort and we started going down faster.

I had never fought a ghost before, not "physically." I

was like some kid on the playground getting in his first fight, not having a clue as to what to do, and flailing around awkwardly.

I increased my efforts and slowed us down, but I wasn't strong enough to stop our descent.

The horizon to the east was starting to lighten as the day dawned. I could see the Ventura Freeway in the distance and the Warner Brothers lot where this all started. I could see the Hollywood sign perched on the craggy hill lit up and declaring for all to see where we were and how grand it must be.

I used to love this town and I used to hate this town. I loved the job, the creation of illusions for entertainment purposes. I hated the town with all the crime and poverty and far too many egos.

Darla was laboring under the illusion that revenge would help. It wouldn't. It would probably lead to the bardo, and from what Banquo once told me back when Haley was trying to exact her revenge, it could lead to an even darker place.

And if I cared enough to try to save Shelia Green's life despite her flaws, shouldn't I try to save Darla's afterlife despite her flaws?

What does one do with a murdering ghost?

I didn't know, so I used my training and improvised.

"Darla, listen to me," I said, whispering to her, hoping that would get her attention. "You can stop now. Eddie is dead and Shelia is ruined. She'll never be the same after this. The shame of her suicide attempt will haunt her for the rest of her life."

"Good," Darla grunted. "She ruined my life."

"Don't kill her, Darla," I said. "You don't really want to kill her."

"Oh, no. Darla does want to kill her." She grunted again and we descended faster.

"Eddie's not a ghost," I said, "but I know that Shelia will be if she dies like this. You pushed her over the edge, she won't move on."

"Darla wanted Eddie to be a ghost," she said with a sniff, our descent halting briefly. "To be her ghost. To start over with Darla again."

She hadn't just wanted to kill him, she wanted him to be with her in the afterlife. The thought almost derailed me. I almost let her go. At first the thought felt so foreign and then I thought about Sun being a ghost and how we could be together again and I understood.

The idea was a siren, the same kind as gambling or propofol used to be. An empty promise that would bring only pain and ruin.

Darla would not have gotten what she wanted if Edward Lincoln had not moved on and become a ghost. It would have made things worse. And I won't get what I want if I haunt Sun waiting for the day she dies and can join me.

The thought was a quick storm in my mind and I came back to myself and renewed my grip on her.

"I'm sorry about that, Darla," I said. "But listen to me. If Shelia becomes a ghost, she will haunt you."

"What!?" she asked, and we were rising again. Below us I could hear the warble of a siren bouncing off the hills as an ambulance rushed to Shelia Green's house.

"Imagine your afterlife, Darla," I said, still whispering to her. "Imagine every day like this, like you and me struggling, like right now. She will know you killed Eddie. She will know you drove her to suicide. She will haunt you. She will follow you. She will not give you a moment of peace."

Our ascent got quicker, Darla barely trying to fly us down anymore, the city growing smaller beneath us again.

"She'll tell you of her passion with Eddie," I whispered. "How they made love, where they made love, how she had loved him the longest and the best. She'll tell you about Eddie and the night he left you for her and what it felt like, what they did, in excruciating detail."

And yes, I was being a real asshole right then. I needed to paint a picture so revolting that Darla would give this up. And while it was only one possible outcome here, it was certainly possible.

"No! Darla doesn't want that."

"How he used to love to come up behind her, pull her lovely hair aside, and kiss her neck," I whispered. "She'll tell you exactly how that felt, how that stood up the hairs on the back of her neck, how that—"

"No! Eddie used to kiss Darla's neck. No! No! No!" Darla intoned and we were flying up twice as fast as before. Darla was flying up too.

"She'll be a ghost," I said. "She'll be able to remember everything perfectly. She'll tell you about it until you beg her to stop and then she'll tell you about it some more."

"Go… go save her," Darla said. She was crying now. "Darla begs you to save her. Darla will leave this awful town. Darla will find a nice quiet place. Darla will be good."

I let her go up there high above Los Angeles. We were high enough that the ocean was just visible to the southwest and the sun was just peaking up above the distant horizon.

Darla stared at me, the fury in her face still clear, but fear too.

"You belong with that wicked old woman that looks

like a little girl," Darla spat. "Darla thinks you are wicked too and that Emily is perfect for you."

The accusation stung because there was some truth to it. But I did what I had to do to save a life.

Darla looked down at the city below us and shook her head, her lip curling into a sneer. She looked up at me and shouted. "Go! Go save the horrible Shelia Green. Let her live without Eddie. Darla thinks now that that is punishment enough."

With that she flew to the north and I flew down to do as she asked.

Chapter Fourteen

THAT WAS THE LAST WE SAW OF AMANDA DARLA YORK. I asked Tamara to look into her and a quick google search revealed that Darla had overdosed on... you guessed it, vodka and sleeping pills. I don't quite understand it, but Darla had figured out how to infect Shelia Green with her own depression, had tried to give Shelia her own death.

Darla and Eddie's baby was now with Darla's parents. He was only twenty months old, so maybe with their love and the support of Eddie's estate the kid would have a decent life.

We stayed with Shelia Green for three more days, pumping her full of warmth. It wasn't pretty, those days in the ICU. She almost died two times. We're talking a crash cart, and shocking her heart, and all that mayhem.

It got so I had to wonder if we were doing the right thing, if her biology was damaged enough that we should just let her go. And there is no easy answer here. I guess it got kind of personal for me. I didn't want her overdose, influenced by Darla like it was, to turn into what looked like a suicide.

It may seem like a silly distinction. Dead is dead, right? But it's not for the people that loved her. It matters. And while I was no longer sure that my own death was a murder, it could have been an accidental suicide, I knew without a doubt that Shelia Green was under the influence of Darla, and what happened wasn't really her choice.

So we stayed and we fought for her survival.

I think it was a little bit healing for Emily and me, too. Being in the flow of the warmth that long, constantly letting go, coming back to that lovely sensation was just what we needed.

We didn't talk much, we just kept our hands on her and let the warmth flow. It was like a meditation retreat... except for all the nurses and doctors and beeping machines and IV bags.

When Shelia woke up, when it was clear that she was going to be okay, we only stayed a little longer. Long enough to hear her daughter tell her what happened and promise that she'd be there for her. She had support and that's important whether you're alive or dead.

Emily took my hand and we walked out of the hospital into a bright LA day, an ambulance rushing up with its sirens blaring.

It occurred to me that this could be a valid way to be dead. Hanging out at hospitals and trying to help the living survive whatever kind of trauma had befallen them. Spending your days in the flow of the warmth.

But it wasn't for me.

"Are you okay, Walter?" Emily asked. The lollipop on her shirt was red, but it was a pale red. We were both exhausted and needed to fade, go into that dreamless "sleep" ghosts do from time to time when they are really tired.

I nodded and we kept walking. Something so basic

while you are alive, but pure artifice when you die. But still, walking helps ground you, helps you feel more human. "Are you okay, Emily?"

She smiled, but it wasn't a youthful smile, it was a world-weary smile on her young, round face. "I guess."

Emily had found me this murder, had left me here thinking that this might be what I needed. But it wasn't. Tucson and our graveyard was my home now.

"Um... I..." I began, the words hard to find.

Emily stopped and hopped up onto a low wall that bordered a cheerful flower bed in front of the hulking hospital. She sat down and patted next to her.

I sat down and stared at the cars on the street. "I know I need to follow up on the lead I found, but... I can't. Not yet. I need time."

"You don't have to do it for me, Walter," she said, her lisp a little thicker than usual, another sign of fatigue. "You have to do it for you."

I nodded. "Thank you."

We sat there for a while watching the living flow in and out of the building. Some in wheelchairs, some limping, some clearly injured, and then others walking quickly in scrubs, or concerned family members with worry written on their faces.

"I was wondering something, Emily," I said.

She nodded for me to continue.

"What do you do when we are not... you know..." I nodded towards the hospital. "Dealing with all the murder and mayhem."

She shrugged and cocked her head, her green eyes intense, the lollipop on her T-shirt swirling into a bright yellow. "Why, I like to travel, Walter. Why do you ask?"

I suppressed a laugh. The phrasing of it was so inno-cent on the surface, but it was very clear she liked this avenue of questioning. "Because," I began. "Maybe you and I can do something besides murder. You know, for a change of pace. Something that you like to do."

She smiled and nodded enthusiastically, her blond ringlets bouncing. She hopped off the wall and held out her hand. "I would like that, Walter."

I stood and took her hand and we kept walking. We needed to fade, but we still needed to ground a little more. So we walked away from the hospital and down the busy street, seeing a few homeless people, some joggers, and some pedestrians. Behind us was the hospital with the sick and the dying and here it was just another day in Hollywood.

"Edward Lincoln's funeral is today," Emily said, a mischievous look on her face. "I know we are both tired, but maybe it would help."

It seems strange that we were so tired but still looking for something to do. For the living, this would be needing something calm and normal to do after a particularly harrowing and exhausting day. Like flopping down on the couch and watching a show or two. Something normal. Something fairly mindless. Then you'll be able to go to sleep.

Well, for ghosts, there is little more normal than a funeral.

I nodded and with a "pop" we were in a cemetery, a large crowd gathered, most of the living in black. Behind and above the arrayed living, many of them actors and actresses I recognized, were ghosts. Hundreds of ghosts. Young, old. Short, tall. Slim, fat. Dressed in everything from nightgowns, to modern suits, to clothing that are clearly over a century old.

There were wispy moaning bardoed ghosts that are the cliched version of what the living think of ghosts. There were well-practiced ghosts that were barely transparent, and clearly newbie ghosts that were having trouble keeping their forms solid.

Tall trees surround the granite-filled grassy area, and six pallbearers carried a rather plain wooden coffin on their shoulders.

Emily, still holding my hand, pulled me in line right behind the pallbearers, as if we had an important place in all of this. I saw nods and looks of recognition from the other ghosts as they saw Emily, but the ghosts were as silent as the humans, some sniffing coming from both the living and the dead.

Emily had clearly been here before. In her over eighty years dead, she's probably been everywhere.

I looked down and caught her eye and she gave me a tight smile and a nod.

It gave me hope. It made me think that the two of us were going to be okay. And maybe by asking her to do something else with me besides murder, she wanted to open up, wanted to show me this whole other community of ghosts.

We followed the somber procession through the hundreds of living and hundreds of dead until we got to the gravesite and the casket was placed on the metal frame that will lower it into the ground and take the remains of Edward Lincoln six feet under.

We stood there while a Catholic priest, dressed in white, spoke, while ghost after ghost walked up to the casket, reached in to touch Edward Lincoln's corpse and whispered their goodbyes.

And I recognized some of these ghosts. The faces you see during the Oscar's In Memoriam segment. I was starstruck in the presence of some of them. Oscar winners and some of my acting heroes long gone.

Not to mention the living. There were a slew of Emmy winners and a few Oscar winners among them. I had been in Hollywood a while and never been around this density of stars.

I caught Emily's eyes after a very famous actress, dead ten years now, said her very tearful goodbyes. Emily threw me a brief grin and squeezed my hand, and in that moment I realized something.

I don't deserve Emily. How could I? She could be anywhere hanging out with any ghosts she wanted. The former rich and the former famous. Or the brilliant and insightful. Or the most interesting storytellers this world's earthbound spirits has to offer. But she chooses to hang out with me. Over and over.

I don't deserve her.

I opened my mouth to speak, to say something about this realization, but Emily put her finger to her young lips and whispered, "Wait for it."

I looked around. What could be coming?

The priest was finishing the service saying something in Latin that sounded quite regal. A prayer, many heads, both living and dead, bowed.

When he snapped his bible shut, there was a collective intake of breath from the dead.

A spirit was rising out of Edward Lincoln's coffin. A ghost. A Hollywood handsome man in his sixties with salt and pepper hair and a cleft chin. The spirit was "dressed" in an expensive three-piece suit.

"What?" I asked.

Emily shrugged. "Sometimes it takes a while for the soul to separate. Sometimes a long time."

I smiled and shook my head. This was what Darla wanted, but she missed it. I watched as the new ghost of Edward Lincoln was welcomed into his new community.

Gently. Slowly. Each ghost taking their time, trying not to shock him into the bardo.

It takes a village to raise a ghost properly and this group of ghosts knew what they were doing. They got him moving. Got him talking. Distracted him from the living and the coffin being lowered into the ground.

After the living wandered off, the dead really started the party. I met ghost after ghost and found their greeting ritual is the same as ours back in Tucson.

"Hello, my name is Walter Anchor and I died when someone overdosed me with propofol."

I met stars and fellow grips and plenty of regular old people. All like me with unfinished business. All in search of an afterlife worth living.

Hours later, Emily and I were finally alone again.

"Thank you," I said.

"Sure," she said with a nod. "Lots of your people here."

I shook my head. "No, Emily. My people are in Tucson." She opened her mouth to speak, but I continued. "Don't get me wrong. This has been great, and I'd love to hang out here some, but my home is with you and Blinky and Anna-Marie and Fredrick and... even Banquo."

She swiped her forehead dramatically, pantomiming great relief. "Glad you got that figured out."

This whole thing had been her trying to help me. I didn't deserve her, but I was dedicated to doing better.

But it was a strange dichotomy. I needed to get the courage up to follow the lead, find out if my former dental assistant was involved in my death *and* I needed to pay more attention to the needs of my friends and not make this afterlife all about solving murders... especially mine.

My life had been a strange dichotomy, actor and then dentist, so why not my afterlife?

"You know," I said with a smile. "*Annie* is playing on Broadway. Maybe New York would be fun. We could see some shows."

Emily smiled broadly and I caught a wicked glint in those green eyes of hers. "And maybe," she said, "we'll just stumble onto a murder and…" She ended with an exaggerated shrug.

I had to laugh. Emily so loves murder.

More Mystery?

WALTER AND EMILY HAVE A LOT MORE CASES TO SOLVE. Next is **"The Red Arrow Murders,"** available September, 2020. Join my email newsletter and never miss a thing.

The Red Arrow Murders

Walter Anchor spends his afterlife solving murders in the hope of one day solving the toughest murder of all. His own.

But when he and his partner and best ghost-friend Emily stumble upon a series of murders committed for a ghost to find, for Walter and Emily to find, everything changes. Can he face the reality of his own death, save the woman he still loves, and do the unthinkable before anyone else dies?

From the author of *Shuffled Off: A Ghost's Memoir* comes a mystery unlike anything seen before.

Get "The Red Arrow Murders" Now!

About the Author

Robert J. McCarter is the author of seven novels, three novellas, and dozens of short stories. He is a finalist for the *Writers of the Future* contest and his stories have appeared or are forthcoming in *The Saturday Evening Post, Pulphouse Fiction Magazine, Fiction River, Andromeda Spaceways Inflight Magazine,* and numerous anthologies.

His latest effort is a serialized novel called *Woody and June Versus the Apocalypse*, a story of adventure and love and taking things (even the apocalypse) in stride. Of his novel, *Seeing Forever*, Kirkus Reviews says, "Sci-fi as it should be: engaging, moving, and grand in scope."

He lives in the mountains of Arizona with his amazing wife and his ridiculously adorable dogs.

Find out more at:
robertjmccarter.com

Books by Robert J. McCarter

Walter Anchor, Ghost Detective Stories

- **Case 1: Detecting Haley** (also part of *Life After: Stories of Life, Death, and the Places in Between*)
- **Case 2: The Ghost Bride's Gift**
- **Case 3: A Long Hard Fall**
- **Case 4: Death of a Dentist**
- **Case 5: A Hollywood Kind of a Murder**
- **Case 6: The Red Arrow Murders** (coming September, 2020)
- **Unfinished Business: The Cases of Walter Anchor Ghost Detective** (coming October, 2020)

For a complete list of Walter Anchor stories, go to RobertJMcCarter.com/WalterAnchor

Novels in the "Ghost's Memoir" world:

- Shuffled Off: A Ghost's Memoir, Book 1
- Drawing the Dead
- To Be a Fool: A Ghost's Memoir, Book 2
- Of Things Not Seen: A Ghost's Memoir, Book 3
- A Boy, a Girl, and a Ghost

For a complete list the "Ghost's Memoir" novels, go to ShuffledOff.com

The Woody and June versus the Apocalypse Series

Find out more at WoodyAndJune.com

The Neutrinoman and Lightningirl Series

Find out more at Neutrinoman.com

Other Novels:

- Seeing Forever

For a more information, go to RobertJMcCarter.com